MADAME PAMPLEMOUSSE
and the Time-Travelling Café

Also by Rupert Kingfisher

Madame Pamplemousse and Her Incredible Edibles

MADAME PAMPLEMOUSSE
and the Time-Travelling Café

BY Rupert Kingfisher

ILLUSTRATED BY
Sue Hellard

BLOOMSBURY
LONDON BERLIN NEW YORK

For Rosie and the Caterpillar

Bloomsbury Publishing, London, Berlin and New York

First published in Great Britain in 2009 by Bloomsbury Publishing Plc
36 Soho Square, London, W1D 3QY

A CIP catalogue record of this book is available from the British Library

ISBN 978 1 4088 0054 6

Typeset by Dorchester Typesetting Group Ltd
Printed in Great Britain by Clays Ltd, St Ives plc

3 5 7 9 10 8 6 4

www.bloomsbury.com/childrens

Chapter One

In the city of Paris, in the district of Montmartre, at the top of a steep, winding hill, there is a café. An old-fashioned and elegantly furnished café, with polished wooden tables, frosted-glass windows and an awning of striped gold and green.

Inside, the walls are adorned with posters: vintage advertisements for drinks from ages past, such as Mermaid Madeira, Green Fairy Liqueur, Dark Horse Chocolate and Red Devil Lemonade.

Other strange-looking antiques are distributed all around – pieces of marble and old statues, carved figureheads and masks – giving the café the appearance of a small museum. And this is perhaps how it acquired its title: The Café of Lost Time.

However, the true reason for its name is a secret, a secret housed within the gleaming, silver steam-powered espresso coffee machine sitting atop the café bar.

The machine was invented by the café's owner, whose name is Monsieur Moutarde. Moutarde was once a famous scientist, a professor at the university, who resigned from his professorship quite suddenly one day, after making the most remarkable discovery.

The discovery came to him on a Sunday afternoon while out with his nephew and niece. They were looking round the dinosaur gallery in the Museum of Natural History, when Monsieur Moutarde paused to admire the skeleton of a diplodocus.

There was something about its mere presence there that never ceased to amaze him – how this was no replica but the actual bones of a creature that had once walked the Earth, many millions of years ago. And yet here it was standing right next to him.

Afterwards they went to a café where Monsieur Moutarde ordered a particular kind of orange-flavoured cake that had been a favourite of his as a child. He had not eaten one since and only ordered it on a whim. But at the first taste he had such an intense memory of childhood that, for a second, he actually believed himself back in the past.

 'Eureka!' he exclaimed, suddenly leaping from his chair. The other people in the café looked up warily, although his niece and nephew didn't bat an eye, for they were used to this sort of behaviour from their uncle.

'That's it!' he cried euphorically, pacing briskly up and down. 'The taste brings back the memory, just like you're really there. So you'd only have to trick the universe into agreeing with your senses and . . . *sacré bleu!* Why, then you would have time travel!'

'Except it wouldn't work!' he explained later, dejectedly, to a friend. 'Tricking the universe is no problem – that's the easy part – but it would only work with your own memories. What about times you've never experienced?

Or times before human beings even existed?'

His friend shrugged. 'Surely it's only a matter of imagination?' she said.

'Well, yes, of course, but an imagination of genius!'

'That shouldn't pose too much of a problem,' said his friend. And indeed, for her, it would not, since her name was Madame Pamplemousse, and she was the greatest culinary genius the world has ever known.

So together they invented the Taste-Automated Space-Time Déjà-Vu Generator. Monsieur Moutarde designed the machine, while Madame Pamplemousse devised the recipes – special blends of ingredients whose flavours vividly recalled the past. These ingredients would then be fed into the Generator, where they would be subatomically blended with quantum froth and spritzed with space-time foam. Finally, the resulting liquid would be dispensed into a cup and look much like a small black coffee. Except that whoever drank this liquid would be transported through time and space.

No sooner had they built the machine, however, than they realised the potential dangers of their discovery. For who knew what terrible uses it might be put to if the Generator fell into the wrong hands?

So Madame Pamplemousse and Monsieur Moutarde chose to hide it. Given its remarkable similarity to a coffee machine, Moutarde had the ingenious idea of concealing it inside a café. And so he resigned from his position at the university and became a café owner instead.

The café actually did quite well and acquired something of a reputation throughout Paris. This was partly due to its unusual decor and museum-like appearance, and partly due to the strange rumours it attracted.

It was widely believed, for example, that the café was haunted. For there were reports of people glancing through the windows at night, and seeing figures inside who would then mysteriously vanish before their eyes. Or there was another, particularly fanciful story

from someone claiming to have seen a cat standing on its hind legs and leaning against the bar. The cat had also, apparently, worn an eyepatch and had been sipping an apéritif.

Madame Pamplemousse ran a shop called 'Edibles' on the banks of the river, just off the main street down a narrow, winding alley. It was a small and rather unremarkable-looking shop but, in fact, sold some of the most extraordinary food ever tasted.

It had, for example, several hundred different cheeses, some of them dating back many centuries. One in particular was so oozing and putrid that it had to be kept chained up beneath a thick marble lid.

Among the giant cured meats hanging from the ceiling there was Smoked Pterodactyl Wing, Salted Ichthyosaur Fin and Triceratops Tail with Garlic. All around the walls, winding up to the ceiling, there were shelves packed with jars and tiny bottles, with their contents written on the labels in fine, purple script: Pickled Tarantula Legs in Tarragon Vinegar, Black Mamba Tongues in Red Wine, Peppered Dragon Spit with Fairy-Ring Mushroom and Kraken Tentacle with Rose-Petal Jam.

She also sold one particular delicacy which had neither a name nor any ingredients on the label. This was because the ingredients were a secret, for it was The Most Incredible Edible Ever Tasted.

Madame Pamplemousse lived above the shop with her cat, Camembert, a stray who had wandered in off the streets one night, after being involved in a fight. During the fight, Camembert had nearly died and lost one of his eyes, but Madame Pamplemousse had nursed him back to health. And ever since they had lived together very happily. They would run the shop by day and, come sundown, would often share a bottle of Violet-Petal Wine on Madame Pamplemousse's balcony above the city. And often they might be joined by their good friend Madeleine.

Madeleine was a girl who lived nearby above a restaurant called the Hungry Snail. She had recently been adopted by the restaurant's owners, Monsieur and Madame Cornichon. This was only one of the incredible things that had happened to Madeleine since stumbling across Madame Pamplemousse's shop. Another was that she herself had been discovered as an exceptionally talented cook.

However, this did have the slight drawback that Madeleine was regularly hounded by the press and television companies trying to persuade her to appear on children's cookery shows. These offers she would always decline, preferring instead to remain anonymous. But she could not prevent people from

taking her picture and printing it in the
newspapers. And this is why, bright and early
one morning, she received a visitor at the
Hungry Snail.

Chapter Two

Sometimes Madeleine could hardly believe her luck, for it was only last summer that her whole life had changed.

No longer did she have to live with her parents, which was just as well, since they had spent most of their time trying to get rid of her. Nor did she have to spend every holiday scrubbing dishes in her uncle's restaurant.

Instead, Madeleine lived with the Cornichons in their apartment above the Hungry Snail. The restaurant had been re-decorated according to Madame Cornichon's instructions, and was full of light and space and fresh flowers. It was the sort of place that made you happy just by being there. Monsieur Cornichon devised the menus – although Madeleine was his chief consultant – and each week they would discuss what new recipes to include.

But from the time Madeleine used to live

with her parents, she had developed a sort
of rule or principle about the universe. And
this rule stated: *whenever you begin to
really enjoy yourself, someone will always try to
stop you.*

She had even tested this law scientifically
and found that whenever she performed some
boring activity, such as homework or brushing
her teeth, she would be left in perfect solitude.
But the moment things took a more interest-
ing turn, some adult would be there, telling
her to stop.

It turned out that Madeleine's Law was,
indeed, as universal as she supposed. For last
summer had been memorable for everyone
in Paris, not for any special reason, just a

general feeling in the air, a sense that things were possible where they had not been so before. But as the days got colder and the nights drew in, the President of France decided everyone had been having too much fun and that it was time to bring it to an end.

The President hated Paris. He loathed it with a passion. To him it seemed a lazy, slovenly city, where people did nothing but eat and talk and fall in love when they should have been doing something far more practical, like cutting down rainforests, instead. And so he began planning Paris's systematic destruction.

All of the city's older and more beautiful

architecture was set for demolition, with hideous new buildings to be put up in its place. All of the parks, art galleries and museums were sold off to become shopping centres, and all the small, independent shops and restaurants were to be closed, to make way for multinational chains. And in these chain restaurants strict time limits would be imposed on how long people were allowed to dine. Gone were the days when you could spend whole afternoons having lunch, and dancing the night away was now strictly forbidden.

The minister responsible for administering these new laws was the President's second in command: a young woman by the name of

Mademoiselle Fondue. And it was she who, early one Saturday morning, was knocking on the restaurant door.

Madeleine was still in bed when she heard the knocks. She had been lying there half asleep, drifting in and out of dreams, when the sound woke her with a start.

Quickly, she got dressed and hurried down the stairs. The restaurant was deserted, with all the chairs stacked up on the tables from the night before. She made her way through the empty dining room and opened the front door.

Outside she found a young woman, dressed smartly in a plain black suit. She was very pretty and looked like a model or film star, with glossy blonde hair and dazzling white teeth.

'Good morning,' she said, smiling brightly.

'Good morning, Madame,' said Madeleine.

'I'm here to see Monsieur and Madame Cornichon. Are they in?'

'No, I'm afraid not. But they should be back soon.'

'Ah, well,' she said, breezing straight through the door. 'Then perhaps I might come in and wait.'

Madeleine showed her to a table. 'Would you like a coffee or something?'

'Coffee!' said the woman disdainfully.

'No, thank you, I don't drink coffee. A bottled mineral water will do fine.'

Madeleine went to fetch the water. The woman, meanwhile, opened her briefcase and took out an official-looking file.

'So, you must be the Cornichons' daughter?' she said. She took the water from Madeleine without offering any thanks.

Madeleine shook her head. 'Not really. I'm their adopted daughter.'

'I see. Great. And I suppose it must be fun living above a restaurant?'

'Yes, it is.'

'You must do a lot of cooking?'

'Um . . . yes,' said Madeleine warily.

'Occasionally, now and again.'

The question had instantly raised Madeleine's suspicions. Before now, journalists had tried to sneak their way into interviews uninvited. This woman might easily be a journalist in disguise.

'Because, of course,' said the woman, 'you're something of a celebrity, aren't you, Madeleine? "Paris's new gastronomic star."'

On hearing this, Madeleine froze.

For a start, the woman had used her name, which Madeleine had never given her. But she had also directly quoted from a newspaper article written about Madeleine last summer.

'Excuse me,' said Madeleine, 'but who exactly are you, Madame?'

The woman smiled. 'My name is Mademoiselle Fondue and I work for the government.'

'The government?'

'That is correct.' The woman motioned with her eyes for Madeleine to sit down. Madeleine obeyed. 'Now, Madeleine, I understand you don't much enjoy your celebrity and that you have consistently avoided talking to the press, is that right?'

Madeleine nodded.

'And that you also refuse to take part in televised cookery shows?'

Madeleine nodded.

'And why is that?'

'Because I don't want to.'

Mademoiselle Fondue frowned. 'I don't understand – you don't like cooking?'

'No . . . no, I like cooking.'

'Of course you do. In fact, you love it. It's your great passion. So why don't you want to share that passion on national television?'

Madeleine ransacked her brain, trying to think of a reply. The truth was she preferred not to discuss her gift for cookery. She feared that doing so might ruin it somehow, like a plant that prefers the shade being given too much sun. However, she also knew, instinctively, that a woman like this would never understand such an answer, and so she tried to think of an alternative.

'Because I don't want to,' she said eventually.

Mademoiselle Fondue grinned, shaking her head. 'Uh-uh. Not good enough, Madeleine. By refusing to sell your talent, the television companies lose out. They lose large sums of money, which, in turn, makes you a drain on the economy and that's now a very serious crime.'

She allowed the full shock of this to sink in before continuing. 'However, that isn't my main reason for visiting you today.' From out of the file she produced a newspaper cutting. 'I am here,' she said, 'because your name has

 been associated with a peculiar sort of urban myth. A myth about a certain legendary foodstuff.'

She passed the newspaper cutting across the table. It was another headline Madeleine recognised from last summer, which read:

THE MOST INCREDIBLE EDIBLE EVER TASTED: WAS IT REALLY ALL A HOAX?

'We believe you have information about this Edible,' said Mademoiselle Fondue. 'And about its possible creator – a woman by the name of Madame Pamplemousse.'

Madeleine's heart felt like it had just fallen through the floor. 'Wh-who?' she stammered.

Mademoiselle Fondue smiled, cocking her head to one side. 'Madame Pamplemousse. Your friend who runs the food shop in the Rue d'Escargot. The one I've recently had set for demolition.'

'But you can't!' Madeleine blurted out without thinking.

Mademoiselle Fondue smiled coolly. 'Oh, so you *do* know her? Well, Madeleine, on the contrary, I have just the power to do such a thing. And that is why I suggest you tell me everything you know about this woman, including her possible location.'

Madeleine looked down at her lap. She was trying her best to remain calm. Her only hope in this otherwise dreadful situation was the fact that the government didn't know where her friend was. And neither, as it happened, did Madeleine. She hadn't seen Madame Pamplemousse or Camembert for well over a week now.

'I don't know where she is,' she said finally.

'Really?' said Mademoiselle Fondue. 'Well, perhaps it will come to you in a little while – after spending some time in your new home.' She grinned, showing off her perfect teeth. 'A detention centre for Paris's worst child criminals. And a place where, incidentally, should I so decide it, you will be spending the rest of your childhood.'

Chapter Three

Just then the door opened and the Cornichons walked in. They had been shopping at the fish market that morning and were carrying large boxes of seafood.

'Good morning, Monsieur and Madame!'

said Mademoiselle Fondue brightly. 'Allow me to introduce myself – my name is Mademoiselle Fondue and I work for the government.' She showed them her identi-fication. 'I'm here to take Madeleine into custody.'

For a stunned moment, the Cornichons stared at her in silence. Then together they dropped their boxes with a crash.

'What?' said Madame Cornichon. 'But I don't understand; the adoption papers are all in order. We've done nothing wrong!'

'Really?' said Mademoiselle Fondue. 'Then what about Madeleine's behavioural problems?'

'*Behavioural problems?*' Madame Cornichon

cried. 'What on earth do you mean?'

'Well, for example, Madeleine's refusal to appear on cookery shows despite repeated offers to do so – behaviour which has caused television companies to lose a great deal of money.'

'So?' said Monsieur Cornichon, with a shrug. 'Who cares if a few television companies lose money?'

Mademoiselle Fondue regarded him coldly. 'Well, I do, Monsieur. And so does the government. That's why Madeleine's failure to cooperate is now considered a crime.'

Madame Cornichon gasped with horror, covering her mouth with her hands. Her husband, however, began to seethe.

'How dare you,' growled Monsieur

Cornichon. 'You fascist pig! How dare you come in here and start ordering us around!'

He carried on like this, shaking his fist and shouting louder all the time, until there was a sudden bang and the door swung open.

Two dark-suited men swept into the room. They were both tall and muscular and had the look of hardened criminals, even though they were, in fact, secret police. With alarming speed, they seized hold of Monsieur Cornichon about the arms and wrestled him, still shouting, to the ground.

'No! Don't!' Madeleine screamed. 'Don't hurt him! Please!'

There was a silence. Madame Cornichon was sobbing, clutching Madeleine tightly to her chest. But Madeleine gently broke free from her embrace.

'It's all right,' she said. 'I'll come quietly. Only, please, let him go.'

Mademoiselle Fondue gave a nod and Monsieur Cornichon was released.

'Thank you,' said Madeleine. 'And also . . . if I could just fetch my teddy bear? He's upstairs in my room.'

Madeleine was escorted upstairs by one of the policemen. She asked politely if she might be allowed a moment with Teddy by herself. The policeman gave her one minute and said he would be waiting outside the door.

Once alone in the room, Madeleine took a deep breath and then went over to the bedside table. She opened the drawer and took out a small box of matches. This she placed in her pocket. Then she stepped on to her bed, where she lifted herself up on to the window ledge. And then she opened the window and climbed out.

The box of matches had arrived in her possession the week before, under mysterious circumstances.

At weekends, Madeleine sometimes helped out as a waitress at the Hungry Snail. She had become rather good at this and took pride in the number of plates she could carry simultaneously, without dropping a single one.

Last Saturday, she had earned an unusually

large tip. It had come from a distinguished-looking gentleman, who sat quietly by himself in the corner of the restaurant. He looked like he might be some kind of university professor.

'Thank you very much, Monsieur,' she said, reaching to take the money. But as she did so, he placed a small box of matches in her hand. She glanced down at the box. It had written on it the name and address of a café in Montmartre.

'If ever you are in trouble, Mademoiselle,' he said softly, 'then come to my café. You will be most welcome there.'

Then he nodded politely and got up to go. But just as he was leaving, he turned to remark over his

shoulder, 'People like us should stick together, Mademoiselle.'

◦◦◦◦◦

After climbing out of her bedroom window, Madeleine jumped down on to the roof below. The roof was slanted with a perilous drop beneath, but there was a narrow strip of stone running right along its edge. You could only walk along this by placing one foot in front of the other, and this she did, very carefully, while trying not to look down. Madeleine knew she wouldn't have long; by now the secret policeman would be getting suspicious. Hardly believing what she was doing, she broke into a run.

Abruptly, the row of houses came to an end.

She looked about in panic. Some way further below there was a balcony. It was a long way down but she guessed that she could probably make it if she lowered herself halfway. She clambered over the rooftop, clinging on to the ledge by the tips of her fingers until she felt ready to let go.

The fall was further than she had thought and the shock of it sent shooting pains through the soles of her feet. But no sooner had she landed than she heard a scream. The balcony windows were open, and inside a man and a woman were eating breakfast. It was the woman who had screamed and she was staring aghast at Madeleine. Then the man started shouting and waving his arms around. He got up from the breakfast table, but Madeleine bolted straight past him, running out through their front door.

She flew down the stairs and out into the street. She continued running until she reached the Métro and then ran down into the subway.

A train was just pulling into the station and Madeleine jumped aboard. She looked about to see if she had been followed, but there was no sign of the policemen. She breathed a deep sigh of relief. The doors slammed shut and the train rattled off into the tunnel.

Chapter Four

On the back of the matchbox there was a small map showing the café's location. Coming out of the Métro, Madeleine followed the map, climbing up a steep stairway to the top of a hill. This led on to the most famous square in Montmartre, near to the Sacré Coeur cathedral. The café was just off the square, down a little side street.

She pushed open the frosted-glass door. Immediately she could see why it had been called the Café of Lost Time, for the whole place was cluttered with antiques. The walls were decorated with vintage posters. One showed a tiny mermaid inside a bottle of Madeira. Another showed a horse sitting outside a café, wearing a hat and coat and sipping hot chocolate.

'Good day, Mademoiselle,' said a voice softly, just behind her.

She glanced round to see an elegantly whiskered man wearing a pair of pebble glasses. It was the same man who had given her the matchbox. He gestured to a seat at one of the tables and Madeleine sat down.

'You have the matches?' he asked.

She produced them from her pocket.

He smiled. 'Good. Now would you kindly put them back in your pocket.'

She did as he instructed.

'Very good. Now, allow me to introduce myself: my name is Moutarde. I believe we have a certain mutual friend in common.'

'Madame Pamplemousse?' Madeleine said eagerly.

He put a finger to his lips, cautioning her to be silent. 'She

is away at present,' he said under his breath. 'But before she left, she told me to keep watch on you, in case you ever came to any trouble. I take it you are in trouble, Mademoiselle?'

Madeleine nodded.

'Government? Secret police?' He spoke the words lightly, but with the air of a man who has often come up against such authorities.

She nodded again.

'Then we do not have much time. The government has placed cameras all across the city, even on the Eiffel Tower itself. Your journey here has almost certainly been recorded. Please stay right there, I won't be a moment.'

He moved swiftly across the room, over

towards the bar, where there was a large, silver espresso coffee machine.

Madeleine noticed how this was rather more elaborate than conventional coffee makers. It had a large number of levers and dials, and Monsieur Moutarde appeared to be taking great care in adjusting each one. Eventually, he switched the machine on, producing a low humming sound and a large cloud of steam.

When he came back he was carrying a tray. On the tray were three items: a small cup of coffee, a red Thermos flask and what appeared to be a firework.

He pointed to the cup of coffee.

'In a moment you must drink that and drink it straight down. And as you are drinking, you must keep a tight hold of both the firework and the Thermos flask. You must not release them from your grasp – *that is absolutely vital!* For as soon as you have drunk the coffee, strange things will start to happen. All of this will vanish.'

He waved a hand about the room.

'It will disappear before your eyes. And then you will find yourself somewhere totally different. Somewhere very strange indeed. But do not be alarmed. Simply place the firework in the ground, light it very carefully and then remain exactly where you are. Do you understand?'

Madeleine shook her head. 'I'm sorry,

Monsieur,' she said. 'But I don't.'

'The firework is a signal flare! It will show where you can be found. So once you have set it off you must not move from your position. However . . .' His brow furrowed with anxiety. 'If anything should go wrong, if the firework does not work, or, for whatever reason, you find yourself in danger, simply drink that.'

He pointed to the flask.

'Drink it straight down and it will you bring you right back.'

'Bring me back?' asked Madeleine. 'Back from where?'

But just then they were interrupted by a voice from across the room.

'Bad luck, Madeleine,' said Mademoiselle Fondue, coming through the café door. 'Our cameras are much too clever to let anyone get away. I personally supervised their production.' She turned to the two secret policemen beside her. 'Arrest her!' she commanded.

Madeleine jumped to her feet.

'Now!' Monsieur Moutarde whispered.

Remembering his instructions, Madeleine grabbed hold of the firework and Thermos flask and then drank the coffee straight down.

Except that it wasn't coffee. It certainly was hot and dark and looked just like an espresso, but the flavour was totally different.

The feeling of déjà vu is like an experience you've had before, either in a memory or dream. And that was how it felt on first tasting the liquid, as if, for an instant, she were revisiting a dream – a dream about the Earth many millions of years ago, long before human beings existed.

That was when the room began to move.

At first, everybody stopped still, as if captured in a snapshot. It was an eerie sight to behold and, for a moment, Madeleine had the bizarre notion they were all playing some sort of game, pretending to be statues. She could see Mademoiselle Fondue with her mouth open, having just ordered her arrest. And she could see the policemen in mid-stride, frozen halfway across the room. But then this image began revolving, moving faster and faster until

Madeleine feared she might be sick. Soon the room became a whizzing blur, then just a wheel of spinning colour.

Gradually this colour changed to blue. It was of an especially deep, azure shade, and only after she had been staring at it for some time did Madeleine realise that she was looking at the sky.

Chapter Five

It was like stepping into a greenhouse or a bathroom full of steam. The air was hot and sticky and clung about Madeleine's skin. A bright sun was beating down through the cloudless blue sky.

She was standing in the middle of a tropical marshland. The earth was muddy and clay-like. There were clumps of bracken everywhere and coarse bushes and odd, squat little palm trees in the shape of pineapples. She could see water in the distance – a still lake, and beyond that an open plain stretching out for miles towards a mountain range on the horizon.

Then Madeleine turned round and saw the forest.

She was standing right on its edge and it loomed up above her, with trees taller than any she had ever seen. There were palm trees the height of buildings, and what looked like Christmas trees but with gigantic long trunks.

The forest floor itself was covered as densely as a jungle: a thick tangle of high ferns and rope-like hanging vines.

She had not the slightest idea where she was or quite how she could have got there. But she became increasingly aware of the deep silence all around. It seemed to hang suspended, like the moisture in the air, and made Madeleine distinctly uneasy.

She glanced down. The firework was in her hand but not the Thermos flask. She had been holding the flask when she had drunk the liquid, she felt sure. But then the room had started spinning and after that everything was a blur.

That was when she felt her first serious stab

of panic, for Monsieur Moutarde had expressly told her to keep hold of the flask. He had also said something about it 'bringing her back', though she had no idea how. But now it was gone. Somewhere in transit, she had lost it.

Hurriedly, she set about looking for a patch of firm ground. The firework was a sky-rocket, with a long wooden stem, and she pushed this into the clay-like soil. She reached into her pocket. Relieved to find the matches still there, she struck one and applied it to the fuse.

For an unpleasantly long time nothing seemed to happen. She didn't know whether to risk lighting it again, and had just decided to do so when there was a sudden fizzing whistle and the rocket shot up into the sky. It went high, high up until it exploded with a bang, raining down in bright blue and gold sparks. The sparks faded out to leave thin traces of smoke, which soon vanished away altogether. But, as they did, Madeleine could see something else moving on the horizon.

It was what appeared to be a flock of birds. They were far away, circling above the mountain range, but at the sight of the firework they had evidently been made curious for they were now coming closer. And Madeleine could see how they were, in fact, quite large birds, as even from this distance their wingspan looked considerable.

Nervously, she glanced around. Out here on the marshland she was completely exposed, the only cover being the nearby forest. But Monsieur Moutarde had told her not to move from her position.

She was startled by the sound of a loud screech above her head. One of the birds had flown free of the flock and was swooping down straight towards her.

Except she could see now it wasn't a bird, but a large, leathery-skinned creature with giant wings the size of boat sails. It had a bony crest atop its head and a long, pelican-like beak, studded with sharp, pointed teeth.

Madeleine turned and ran.

She ran frantically, racing headlong into the forest. The bracken whipped her face as she plunged into the undergrowth. She could hardly see the way ahead, but the thought of that long beak suddenly snatching her up kept her moving rapidly onward. Until she glimpsed a place where she might hide: a dense tangle of vegetation, forming a recess underneath.

She dived down, burrowing in deep, and lay still. She held her breath, listening out intently.

Gradually she became aware that there was no sound of wings. Nothing except for the sounds of the forest: the faint hissing of steam and the dripping of moisture from the leaves.

She peered out from under the thicket.

The trees grew so high and so close together that the forest was cast mostly in gloom. But she saw now how the creature could not have followed her – the gaps between the trees would be too narrow for its wings.

A spot of moisture suddenly landed on Madeleine's head. She spun round.

A gigantic tree trunk rose up above her. She presumed the droplet had come from its leaves, and on closer inspection she noticed how its bark was glistening slightly, as if covered in some kind of sap. There was another drop, closely followed by another.

She looked up sharply, angling her neck – and then made two important discoveries.

The first was that the tree in front of her was not actually a tree, but the body of some enormous animal, an animal that looked uncannily like a Tyrannosaurus rex. The second discovery was that the droplets of moisture on her head were the saliva dripping from its jaws.

These jaws were easily big enough to swallow her whole and were moving down closer, until she could feel the dinosaur's hot breath and she was staring into its reptilian yellow eyes.

There was a sudden blur of white.

It all happened so quickly that Madeleine only caught a glimpse, but it appeared to be some kind of creature swinging from a vine. It grabbed hold of her about the waist and lifted her off the ground.

The creature had seized her with such speed that they swung up very high, almost as high as the tops of the trees, and it was up there, in mid-air, that at last she saw her captor's face: a thin, white face with a patch across one eye.

'Camembert!' she cried.

Chapter Six

Madeleine's relief turned to horror when Camembert suddenly let go of the vine. They plummeted downwards with sickening speed.

She screamed and from the forest below

there came an answering roar. Being robbed of its supper had made the Tyrannosaurus extremely angry. It had positioned itself underneath them, with its jaws opened wide and its little arms gesticulating wildly.

But then once again they were swinging up. Camembert had caught hold of another vine just in time and they swung clear of the Tyrannosaurus's mouth. Then Camembert let go again, to grab hold of another, and so he swung on, moving from tree to tree with the agility of a lemur.

In this way they travelled deep into the forest, with Madeleine clutching on to him all the while, until, finally, Camembert performed one last giant swoop, to bring them into the high branches of a tree.

But across the branches planks of wood had been laid. They had been bound together with vines to form a small platform: a tree house with a high view over the forest.

A gas fire was burning with a pot cooking above it. And there, stirring the pot, was a woman dressed in black. She looked round on hearing them arrive.

'Madeleine!' said Madame Pamplemousse, without missing a beat. 'You're just in time for

supper.' And then she smiled and came over to embrace her.

Together the three of them took soup and, meanwhile,

Madeleine asked questions about the café and the strange liquid and how, exactly, she had got there. Madame Pamplemousse explained about the Generator and how Madeleine had just travelled through time.

'Time travel?' Madeleine cried. 'Then where are we?'

'It's hard to be precise,' said Madame Pamplemousse. 'But if Monsieur Moutarde's calculations are correct, this will one day become North America.'

'But what year are we in?'

'Again, difficult to be precise, but somewhere around the late Cretaceous period, eighty million years before our own time.'

'Eighty million years! You mean that creature

down there . . .' Madeleine pointed down to the forest below, 'that really was a-a –'

Camembert miaowed.

'A Tyrannosaurus rex,' Madame Pample-mousse translated.

Camembert miaowed again.

'He says you were lucky. Tyrannosaurs often wait in ambush for hours at a time. That one was probably very hungry.'

Madeleine shivered all over. 'Eurrgh!' she exclaimed. 'I could feel its breath on my face! I could even feel its saliva in my hair!'

On hearing this, Camembert and Madame Pamplemousse turned to each other sharply.

'What is it?' said Madeleine.

They made no reply but Camembert padded swiftly over to the other side of the tree house and came back dragging a small bag. From out of the bag he removed a jar with a vacuum-sealable lid and a small plastic comb, and with this he then proceeded to comb Madeleine's hair. Afterwards, he opened up the jar and then, running a single claw along the comb's teeth, caused small droplets of liquid to fall into it.

'Is there enough?' asked Madame

Pamplemousse.

Camembert nodded briefly before replacing the jar's seal.

'Excellent!' she said. 'Then,

Madeleine, it would seem your arrival here has already brought us luck!'

Madeleine stared at her in bemusement.

'A most valuable delicacy: the freshly extracted drool from a Tyrannosaurus rex. Camembert and I have just spent this past week trying to obtain it . . .' She broke off, abruptly, noticing Madeleine's expression. 'Is something the matter?' she asked.

For Madeleine's face had suddenly fallen. In the relief of being rescued, and the joy of seeing them again, she had quite forgotten the danger back in Paris. Paris now seemed very far away, as indeed it might, since the city would not be built for another eighty million years. But on hearing Madame Pamplemousse talk about cookery, she was filled with a sudden despair.

'I'm sorry, Madame,' she said quietly. 'But something terrible has happened back home. The woman from the government – the one investigating you – she said they've seized your shop and that it's going to be destroyed!'

Madame Pamplemousse received this news calmly, without appearing in the least bit surprised. 'This woman,' she said, 'not, by any chance, a young woman with excellent teeth and hair, who goes by the name of Mademoiselle Fondue?'

'Yes!' Madeleine cried. 'You know her?'

Madame Pamplemousse nodded. 'Oh yes,

we know her. Camembert has had his eye on her for some time.'

Camembert growled, causing Madame Pamplemousse to burst out laughing.

'Forgive me,' she said. 'But I don't think I'll translate. Suffice it to say he didn't much enjoy her company.'

'But you don't understand! The police are looking for you. If you go back, they'll arrest you immediately!'

'Why, naturally,' said Madame Pample-mousse. 'I'd expect them to do nothing less.'

'But, Madame, you can't . . .' Madeleine's voice faltered. And then, quietly, she added, 'You can't stay *here* for ever.'

Madame Pamplemousse looked down over

the panoramic vista that lay below them. She shrugged. 'I could do a lot worse. At least here you're not bothered by government officials.'

She turned back to Madeleine and smiled. 'No, Madeleine, I won't stay here. Apart from anything else, you can't get a decent cup of coffee. I have no doubt Mademoiselle Fondue is very powerful – second only in power to the President himself, and some would say even more so. But that will also prove her undoing.'

'What do you mean?'

'Never mind that for now. But rest assured Mademoiselle Fondue is the least of our problems. Much more important are those ingredients we have yet to obtain.'

'Ingredients for what?'

'For a kind of medicine, a special tonic – one with which we shall restore the very spirit of our city. For the government is attempting to destroy that spirit, and already it has started to sicken.'

Later that night, they sat out under the stars. It was cooler and less humid at night, and Camembert rolled out a sleeping bag for Madeleine to climb into. Then he went over to the edge of the parapet to keep a lookout for passing pterodactyls.

Madame Pamplemousse, meanwhile, lit her pipe and told Madeleine of their adventures so far, seeking ingredients for the special tonic. She told her how they had been to ancient Peru to acquire a whole Green Demon Pimento, the hottest chilli pepper in existence, how they had been to Revolutionary France to steal some wine from Napoleon's cellar. And she told her how they had travelled to India two and a half thousand years ago to obtain a cup of green tea brewed by the Buddha.

As a young man, the Buddha had sat meditating under a banyan tree and discovered the secret of eternal happiness. When Madame Pamplemousse came to visit him he was much older, around eighty, although on first sight she described seeing a beautiful young prince with eyes like dancing flames. Then she saw how he was, in fact, just an old man wearing a plain, saffron-coloured robe. His eyes, however, were unchanged. The idea of time travel seemed to amuse him and he laughed a good deal. He was also very interested to meet Camembert, treating him with great respect, and suggested the two of them play draughts.

Listening to her voice against the gentle hissing of the gas lantern, Madeleine soon began to feel drowsy. It did not seem to matter that they were up a tree in the middle of a prehistoric forest; with Camembert keeping

watch and Madame Pamplemousse beside her, she would have felt safe anywhere. And so, before the story finished, she had drifted off to sleep.

Chapter Seven

The next morning Madeleine awoke to the sound of hammering. Camembert was banging nails into the tree house and binding the planks together with fresh vines. The remains of last night's camp had been packed away into a large, black rucksack.

Madame Pamplemousse bade her good morning and offered her breakfast, which was a fruit resembling a banana, except that it was coloured bright blue.

'Unfortunately there's no coffee – the greatest hardship of time travel,' she said. 'For at the first taste of French coffee, we would be transported straight back to our own present. However, instead, we have this . . .'

She produced a silver-coloured Thermos flask. It was similar to the kind Monsieur Moutarde had given Madeleine in the café, with a sleek, Swiss look about it: the sort of Thermos you might take up a mountain. Madame Pamplemousse unscrewed the top

and poured out the contents
into three cups.

'Are we ready?' she said to
Camembert.

He was still tinkering with the tree house,
tying up a final knot with a nail between his
teeth. Once he had knocked this into the wood
he looked up and nodded.

'Good,' she said. 'Then it's time we were
moving on. Thanks to you, Madeleine, we
already have our precious drool. But we must
now collect our next ingredient.'

She handed a cup to Madeleine and one to
Camembert. 'Your health!' she said, raising her
cup, and then together they all drank.

It was hot and dark-coloured, like the liquid

from the café, although its flavour was totally different. The immediate effect, however, was similar.

Once again there was that sudden feeling of déjà vu, like an intensely recalled memory or dream. But in this dream Madeleine saw hills encircled by mist and wide expanses of silver-grey water. There was also the faint impression of music from far away, like the distant, mournful wailing of bagpipes.

Then the forest below them began revolving, moving faster and faster, until it became a spinning wheel of green. The sight of it made her so giddy that Madeleine closed her eyes. She tried clinging on to the tree house but then even this began to move. It started wobbling about as if it had come loose and, for one terrible moment, Madeleine thought they might be suspended in mid-air, until she opened her eyes and discovered they were on water.

They were floating in the middle of an enormous lake. The tree house was turning slowly, while gently bobbing up and down – except that, strictly speaking, it was no longer a tree house now, but had become a raft. They were surrounded by a mist, which was drifting in white trails above the surface of the water. The air was cool and fresh, and when Madeleine breathed, her breath formed its own misty vapour.

'Where are we?' she asked.

'The British Isles,' said Madame Pamplemousse. 'Scotland. Loch Ness. And if Monsieur Moutarde's calculations are correct, we should be somewhere around the autumn of the year 1933. Here, you'll need this.' She handed Madeleine a blanket. 'You'll feel the cold soon; your body takes a while to adjust when time travelling.'

Just then Camembert miaowed and in reply Madame Pamplemousse reached into the black rucksack. She took out a length of rope, with a hook attached to one end, and a small glass container. Madeleine recognised this as coming from Madame Pamplemousse's shop, with a yellow label on the jar and something coloured dark red inside it. Madame Pamplemousse opened the jar, which produced a foul fishy odour. She handed it to Camembert, who reached in with his paw and brought out a small, dark piece of flesh. Taking the rope's hook, he stuck it into the piece of flesh and then flung it out into the water. The other end of the rope he tied about his waist.

'Fermented Kraken Kidney,' Madame Pamplemousse explained. 'Extremely rare. I found this one washed up on a beach in Norway. It had started going rotten, but that's fortunate for our purposes, since the monster likes them a bit rancid.'

'Monster?' Madeleine whispered. 'You mean . . . the *Loch Ness monster*?'

Madame Pamplemousse nodded. 'Or, to be more precise, a rare breed of sea serpent that was sighted frequently in these waters in the early 1930s, but has not been seen much ever since.'

'Because it's so shy?' said Madeleine hopefully. 'It's such a shy, gentle creature, that's why it's seen so rarely?'

'Shy?' said Madame Pamplemousse. 'Not really. Elusive perhaps. But also extremely dangerous.' She inhaled sharply, her eyes bright with excitement. 'We are here to acquire a small quantity of its venom. With this venom it stuns its prey, dragging it down to a cave beneath the loch, where it may be consumed at its leisure – a kind of monster's larder, if you will.'

The idea seemed to tickle her and she roared with laughter, but on seeing Madeleine's face, her laughter soon faded. 'Oh, my dear Madeleine,' she said, 'please don't be alarmed. No harm will come to you, I promise.'

Just then Camembert put up his paw to command silence. His ears were pricked up and with his one eye he was staring fixedly ahead.

Madeleine followed his sightline. The mist was now thick about them, a blanket of pure white. But the longer she stared, the more she seemed to spy something lurking beyond the mist: the silhouette of a distant, dark shape.

Then the shape disappeared, but from where it had been there came ripples spreading out across the water. They made the raft wobble slightly when they reached it, but then soon died away until all was still once again.

And then, from underneath, came the most almighty swell.

It lifted up the raft, splitting it asunder and tumbling them head first into the water. Madeleine plunged below the surface. Underneath the water her eyes opened to glimpse a horrible coiled mass of oily, dark skin.

She came up spluttering and gasping for breath. And there, above her, towered the monster.

Its full length would be hard to fathom, since its body was wrapped in coils and kept writhing about the water, churning it into whirlpools. But the neck alone rose up a good three metres high, and she could see a green serpentine head with two fierce, luminous-yellow eyes.

It had bitten deep into the Kraken Kidney but Camembert was still clinging on to the rope's other end. He was hanging from the monster's mouth, while the monster threshed

wildly, swinging him from side to side. But Camembert clung on, twisting the rope about his legs until he was entwined. And then, with a sharp tug, he managed to wrestle the kidney clear and dropped down into the water with a splash. The monster gave a loud hiss from out of its nostrils, and then, plunging its neck downwards, disappeared below the surface in pursuit of him.

'Camembert!' Madeleine screamed. A hand gripped her from behind.

Madame Pamplemousse was clinging on to a piece of raft and she pulled Madeleine in close towards her.

'Madeleine!' she said. 'Listen to me!'

'We have to save him!' Madeleine cried.

'Listen to me!' said Madame Pamplemousse firmly. 'You must do exactly as I say.' She was holding up a dark-green Thermos flask. 'You must drink this now and go on ahead of us –'

'No!'

'We will find you, Madeleine, I promise, but you must go on ahead.'

'But what about Camembert?'

'I can save him but then I can't protect you.'

'I don't care! I'll stay with you!'

'No, Madeleine! Listen – you will find your-self near an island. Swim straight to shore and wait there. Do you understand? Whatever happens, do not move from the shore!'

From underneath, something long and

slippery brushed past Madeleine's leg. She let out a scream.

'Now!' said Madame Pamplemousse.

Madeleine tried to protest but Madame Pamplemousse had already put the flask to her lips. With her other hand she cradled Madeleine's head and tipped the flask back. And then the liquid was on her tongue, trickling down her throat, and a second or so later, she vanished.

Chapter Eight

At first, Madeleine thought the time-travelling liquid had not worked. She had been so afraid for Camembert and so terrified of the monster that she hardly noticed its effects. Added to which, she was still in water, and so did not notice any difference in her surroundings, until she realised the water was now considerably warmer.

Then she saw how the mist had cleared and above her the sky was blue.

She was swimming towards the shore of a small island. It had a long beach of pure, bone-white sand. Veering up from it, there was a rocky hillside strewn with cypresses and olive trees and bushes of wild herbs.

Soon the water became shallower and she was stepping out on to the sand. She looked around.

There was no wind, hardly any tide, and the only sound came from the waves gently lapping against the shore. She stared out across the sea. It lay vast and still, glittering emerald in the sun. But there was no sign of life, no sign whatever of Madame Pamplemousse or Camembert. Her mind began racing: what if the monster got them? What if they had been dragged down to an underwater cave? Or what if they had lost the black rucksack?

This terrible prospect seemed to grow ever more plausible until she was quite certain it must have happened. For, without the time-travelling liquid, there would be no way of them reaching her or, for that matter, ever getting home. They would be stuck in Scotland in 1933, while she would be marooned here on this island.

Just then she heard a sound.

It was only faint, yet loud enough to break the silence. She looked around, trying to find its source, but could find none, the island appearing deserted as before. However, she could have sworn that she heard it.

Then it came again, still faint, but clear and unmistakable this time: it was a woman's voice calling from the hillside.

'*Over here,*' it cried distantly. '*Over here!*'

'I'm coming!' Madeleine shouted and began to run.

The hill was steep and hard to climb, littered with broken rocks and clumps of tangled weeds. But such was her relief at hearing

Madame Pamplemousse's voice that Madeleine managed to scale it in no time.

Then halfway up the hillside she stopped.

Here the landscape flattened out to form a rocky promontory jutting out to sea. There were no shrubs growing, no greenery, and the ground was dusty and scorched. But everywhere she looked there were bones.

She could not tell at first what animals they were from. They were all in shards, scattered around, but she could see bits of shattered ribcage and pieces of broken skull, and each one of them looked suspiciously human.

It was only then she remembered Madame Pamplemousse's warning not to stray from the shore. Perhaps there had been no voice. Maybe it had only been her imagination and all that she had heard was the whistling of the wind.

Except there was no wind and everywhere, she noticed, was eerily quiet. And then she felt that strange pricking sensation down the back of her neck, the feeling that lets you know you're being watched.

She spun round. Ahead, the hill carried on upwards, becoming much steeper and rockier.

And perched just above her, on top of an outfacing crag, was the most terrifying creature she had ever seen.

It had the face of a woman, slender and elegant, with high cheekbones and almond-shaped eyes. It was a face that might have been considered beautiful had it not been covered in black fur. The fur was sleek and glossy and covered its whole body, which she saw to be not human, but the body of a panther, with two velvety wings at its back.

Madeleine had once seen a picture of such a creature in a gallery in Paris, a creature whose name in ancient Greek means 'the strangler', for this was none other than the Sphinx.

The Sphinx was peering down at her and Madeleine could see why it had been so named, since its eyes alone held her paralysed. They transfixed her with their cold malevolence and seemed to see into her very mind.

'What brings you to my island, little one?' asked the Sphinx. Her voice was clear, faintly piercing and yet smooth as silk. And like a silken cord about her throat, with every word it seemed to tighten its hold.

'I-I'm sorry,' Madeleine stammered, trying to avert her eyes. 'I d-didn't mean to intrude.'

'To intrude?' the Sphinx echoed back, dropping down from the ledge with a gentle rustle of her wings. She proceeded to prowl stealthily about Madeleine, her muscular body rippling as it moved. 'Then you came here of your own free will?'

Mute with fear, Madeleine managed to nod.

'That is strange,' said the Sphinx, 'for

usually girl children are brought to me in sacrifice, from parents who wish only to have boys.'

She stopped abruptly in her tracks.

'Ah!' she gasped. 'But your parents *did* give you away, didn't they, Madeleine?' The Sphinx crept closer, peering into her eyes. 'Though you tried so hard to please them. Just as now you fear your friends have abandoned you too.'

The Sphinx licked her lips, gazing at Madeleine in fascination.

'Such a beautiful sadness,' she said. 'I shall enjoy devouring it with relish.'

'Then you'll have to eat us first!' said a voice close behind.

With a whip-like movement, the Sphinx

angled her neck round. And there, standing on the hill's brow, were Madame Pamplemousse and Camembert.

'Very well,' she said. 'As you suggest, I shall eat all three of you.'

'If that is your will,' said Madame Pamplemousse, 'then so be it. This is, after all, your island and we are powerless to resist. But I also know you to be a great lover of riddles, and so before dining, I thought you might like to hear one.'

To this the Sphinx made no immediate reply but appraised Madame Pamplemousse in silence. She stared deep into her eyes, appearing to give her the same sort of scrutiny she had Madeleine.

'Your mind is itself a riddle,' she said eventually. 'And so for one such as yourself, I am prepared to grant this request.'

Madame Pamplemousse bowed her head in thanks and then reached into the rucksack at her back. From out of this she removed a small jar. It was about the size of an egg cup, sealed in wax, with a rough, yellow paper label, upon which nothing was written. Whatever was in the jar appeared to be constantly changing colour, shifting all the while like a forever uncoiling spiral.

Madeleine had seen a jar of its kind before and knew what it contained. It was Madame Pamplemousse's secret recipe, her greatest

creation: The Most Incredible Edible
Ever Tasted.

'Here, then, is your riddle,' said Madame Pamplemousse, opening the jar's seal and placing it on the ground. 'This recipe has many ingredients and yet only one name. That name is a secret. But can you now tell me what it is?'

A second or so passed. The Sphinx was crouched on her hindquarters, staring down at the little jar, when abruptly from her mouth there emerged a long black tongue. She dipped this into the jar, licking up a small quantity, and then moved this ruminatively about her mouth. Until her face became suddenly transfigured.

It was the kind of expression you might have while listening to music, on hearing an unexpectedly haunting phrase. And, for one moment, it looked as if the Sphinx were about to cry.

But instead she opened her mouth and spoke a single word.

Although it was not a word in French or ancient Greek or any mortal language. And its sound was like a thunderclap, splitting apart the sky, and in that instant the whole world seemed to stop.

The scene before Madeleine's eyes lay motionless as in a painting. She saw the emerald-green sea reaching out to the blue horizon, and framed against them she saw the Sphinx: a ruthless and deadly creature whose very being was enigma. But Madeleine could now see this was also what made the Sphinx beautiful, just as the sea is beautiful but also deadly, or the sky both limitless and unknown.

'In the world I come from,' said Madame Pamplemousse, 'somewhere of great beauty is about to be destroyed. It is the place where that Edible is created and with it gone, that Edible will soon lose all its savour. It will come to taste as flavourless as dust. Now, I do not expect any mortal sympathy from you, oh Sphinx, but as you and I do both revere this substance, so I have come to ask of you a boon.'

The Sphinx padded softly over towards Madame Pamplemousse and knelt down. 'I know what it is you wish of me, Madame,' she said, lifting up her head.

And down her cheek there ran a single tear.

Camembert caught the tear within the vacuum-sealable jar. And then, with surprising tenderness, he dried the Sphinx's eye.

❦

Afterwards, the Sphinx offered them food and shelter for the night. This they accepted, although they declined the offer of meat, which was some wind-dried flesh of unknown origin. Instead they ate mountain-goat's cheese, fresh figs and dry, resin-scented wine. And while they ate, Madame Pamplemousse prepared Madeleine for their arrival back in Paris and the danger awaiting their return.

Chapter Nine

Back in the present day, in Paris, in the Café of Lost Time, Mademoiselle Fondue was confused.

Only a minute or so earlier, she had arrived at the café to find Madeleine at one of the tables. But then she had seen Madeleine drink a cup of coffee, and soon after that, she had disappeared. However, Mademoiselle Fondue was not a fanciful person. At school she had excelled in exams and those activities that require intelligence but little imagination. And in general, she trusted only in things that could be precisely quantified and measured. So she did not really believe what she had just seen and assumed it must be her eyes or some trick of the light.

But then something even more perplexing occurred: Madeleine reappeared. Not only that but she looked totally different. Her clothing was torn and covered in sand, and her hair was all matted and tangled.

But Mademoiselle Fondue was also not one to lose control and, if ever she did, she would certainly never show it. So instead she issued a single terse command.

'Seize her!' she barked to the policemen.

One of them grabbed hold of Madeleine by the shoulders, forcing her down into a chair. Mademoiselle Fondue came over to sit down opposite her at the table.

'You should be trying to get into my good books, Madeleine. Because, remember, it's up to me how long you'll be going away.' She grinned, making it sound like she was talking about a holiday camp. 'However, I'm a reasonable person and am prepared to be lenient, provided you tell me everything you can

as to the whereabouts of Madame
Pamplemousse –'

'At your service, Mademoiselle,' interrupted a
voice behind her.

Mademoiselle Fondue looked round to see a
woman in the doorway. She
was dressed in black, carried
a black rucksack, and around
her neck was draped what
looked like a stole, but on
closer inspection, she saw it

was actually a cat: a thin white cat wearing an
eyepatch.

Monsieur Moutarde gave a small nod by
way of greeting. 'Good day, Madame,' he said.

'Good day, Monsieur,' said Madame

Pamplemousse. 'Nice to see you again. You know I've been on holiday?'

'I trust it was relaxing, Madame?'

'Most pleasant, thank you. Despite it being impossible to get a good cup of coffee.'

A brief look passed between them.

'Please take a seat, Madame,' he said, 'and I will fetch you one immediately.'

Madame Pamplemousse sat down at the table. Camembert slunk off her shoulders on to the adjacent chair.

'So,' she said to Mademoiselle Fondue, 'I understand you've been looking for me?'

Mademoiselle Fondue made no reply but instead stared at her coolly. Then she reached into her briefcase and took out a newspaper cutting.

'Perhaps you can enlighten me, Madame,' she said. 'We have been investigating this girl ever since her name became connected with a certain legendary foodstuff so delicious and so extraordinary that it earned a special title.'

She passed the newspaper cutting across the table. It bore the headline:

THE MOST INCREDIBLE EDIBLE EVER TASTED: WAS IT REALLY ALL A HOAX?

'Well?' said Madame Pamplemousse, looking up.

'Well,' said Mademoiselle Fondue, 'you tell me, Madame. Was it all a hoax?'

Madame Pamplemousse stared at her in silence. Mademoiselle Fondue stared back but found that she soon wanted to look away, for there was something unsettling about Madame Pamplemousse's eyes. Their colour alone was unlike any she had ever seen – the deep purple blue of wild lavender. But that was not what she found unnerving – it was the way that they looked so completely unafraid.

'I believe it was a hoax,' said Mademoiselle Fondue quickly. 'I believe you must be using some kind of special chemical additive in your cooking, and I suggest you now tell me what that chemical is.'

There was a long pause.

'And let us suppose for a moment, Mademoiselle,' said Madame Pamplemousse eventually, 'that such a chemical *did* exist . . . then what exactly would you use it for?'

'That information is classified.'

'I see.' Madame Pamplemousse paused. 'So you wouldn't, for example, be using it to control people?'

'Madame,' said Mademoiselle Fondue, with a new edge to her voice, 'you should be aware that we have taken possession of your shop and the moment I give the word, it will be destroyed –'

Madame Pamplemousse interrupted her, lifting up her hand. 'Excuse me, Mademoiselle,' she said, 'but my coffee has arrived.'

Monsieur Moutarde had appeared at the table, bearing a small cup of coffee on a silver tray.

'Madame,' he said, placing it before her.

'Thank you, Monsieur,' said Madame Pamplemousse. She lifted the coffee to her nose, inhaling deeply, and then drank it down in a single gulp. Afterwards she replaced the cup in its saucer, whereupon Camembert began licking the dregs.

Mademoiselle Fondue regarded this with distaste. She was also intensely annoyed at having been interrupted, for nobody had ever done this to her before.

'If you do not cooperate, Madame,' she said, 'then we will not only demolish your shop but the child will be taken into custody, to a children's prison, where she will remain until she turns eighteen. And as for the cat . . .' She flashed a smile in Camembert's direction. 'Well, I think that's best left to your imagination.'

She jumped suddenly in her chair at the sound of a fierce growl. Camembert sprang up on to the table in full attacking stance, with his fangs bared savagely and his hair standing on end.

'Get that cat out of here!' Mademoiselle Fondue shouted.

One of the policemen reached down to grab him but Camembert bit deep into his hand. The policeman screamed. Camembert slipped down under the table and scurried out through the door.

'Mademoiselle,' said Madame Pamplemousse, once the commotion had subsided, 'you are evidently a woman of great intelligence. However, you are wrong in thinking me so sentimental as to care for animals or children.' She waved a hand dismissively at Madeleine. 'Do whatever you wish, I have no further use for her.'

The room fell silent.

Madeleine looked stunned. In fact, she looked devastated, her face a perfect picture of wounded surprise. 'B-but I thought –' she stammered.

'Thought what?' Madame Pamplemousse snapped. 'That you were my *friend*? Don't be ridiculous – you're only a child! You've been nothing to me but a nuisance!'

Madeleine covered her face and started to cry. Madame Pamplemousse, meanwhile, *tsk*-ed irritably and turned back to Mademoiselle Fondue.

'Now, Mademoiselle, you are indeed correct. I do use a secret chemical additive in my cooking, a chemical additive of considerable power.'

In Mademoiselle Fondue's eyes there appeared a small gleam of excitement.

'And on certain conditions . . .' Madame

Pamplemousse paused. 'I would be prepared to let you have it.'

'And what conditions are those?'

'Well, obviously a very large sum of money and, in addition, my own television series.'

Mademoiselle Fondue smiled with quiet triumph. 'Very well, Madame,' she said. 'Then we have a deal.'

'Excellent,' said Madame Pamplemousse. 'I will reveal the chemical formula once the contract has been signed. But for now, I expect you would like to see a small sample?'

Mademoiselle Fondue inclined her head by way of reply.

Madame Pamplemousse reached into the rucksack and took out a vacuum-sealable jar.

'I have the raw materials right here,' she said. 'But in order to make the chemical they must first be passed through a special machine.' She pointed towards the silver coffee machine sitting atop the café bar. 'For now I must reveal to you, Mademoiselle, that this is not just a café but, in fact, a secret laboratory.'

'*Madame!*' Monsieur Moutarde whispered. '*What are you doing?*'

'My apologies, Monsieur,' she said. 'It's been a pleasure working with you but now I'm afraid it's time for me to go it alone.'

Moutarde glared at her. 'Half of that money is *mine!*' he hissed.

Madame Pamplemousse smiled. 'I think

not, Monsieur,' she said, getting up from the table and walking over to the machine. 'The deal is strictly between myself and Mademoiselle Fondue. However, perhaps for old times' sake, you might remind me of the setting? It appears to have slipped my mind.'

In reply, he simply spat at her feet.

'Do as she says!' Mademoiselle Fondue shouted.

The policemen glowered at him menacingly.

'One hundred and six!' said Moutarde under his breath.

'Thank you, Monsieur,' said Madame Pamplemousse.

She opened the vacuum-sealable jar. Its contents were pale green and ever so slightly phosphorescent. But this was not due to any normal chemical reaction, for the jar did not contain the chemicals Madame Pamplemousse had claimed. And even if she had been told its true ingredients, Mademoiselle Fondue would never have believed her. For these ingredients were in fact the freshly extracted drool from a Tyrannosaurus rex, venom from the Loch Ness monster, wine from Revolutionary France, concentrated oil from the Green Demon Pimento, the only tear ever to be shed by the Sphinx and a small cup of green tea brewed by the Buddha.

Madame Pamplemousse emptied the jar's contents into the Generator's giant funnel. Then she pulled a lever, turned each of the dials to 106, and switched on the machine.

Chapter Ten

Outside in the street, round the back of the café, there was a small chimney in the roof. This was connected to the Generator via a system of concealed piping. And a long plume of steam now issued out of it.

The plume rose slowly up into the sky, where it formed a small cloud. This cloud then expanded, spreading out from Montmartre, until it covered the whole city of Paris. And from the cloud there drifted down a light-green-coloured mist.

That was when the first of the strange sightings began.

A group of tourists were out taking photographs of Notre-Dame. They were photographing the gargoyles – the stone demons that decorate the cathedral rooftop.

 But as the mists descended, one of these demons appeared to move. A gargoyle leaning on his elbows, peering down over the

city, suddenly stretched out and yawned.

In the Museum of Natural History, something equally bizarre was taking place. The museum had been closed for redevelopment. Works would soon begin to start turning it into a shopping centre, and the building was full of architects and developers. But all of these people were now running screaming through the doors. Panic had broken out in the Gallery of Evolution, where someone had seen the skeleton of a diplodocus come to life. It had begun swishing its tail, moving its long neck, and appeared to be trying to step down from its pedestal. Then the other prehistoric creatures in the gallery did the same, rattling their bones furiously as if trying to break free, until soon even the pickled specimens in glass cabinets about the walls were shaking their cages and chattering their teeth.

There was also great commotion along the banks of the Seine, for passengers aboard cruise boats had reported seeing a giant sea monster swimming down the river.

In the Louvre Museum, refurbishment had to be suspended after someone claimed to have seen a sphinx jump down out of a painting and go prowling about the corridors.

Meanwhile, at Notre-Dame, a large crowd had gathered at the base of the cathedral, for by now the whole rooftop was swarming with gargoyles.

Like every old building and
monument in Paris, the cathedral
had been set for demolition. A
new steel-and-glass cathedral was
to be put up in its place and so the
whole building was covered in scaffolding. But
the gargoyles were dismantling this, ripping
bits apart and hurling them to the ground.

One of the gargoyles put two fingers in his
mouth and blew a loud whistle. The other
gargoyles looked up. The whistler singled
out two of them, muttering a few guttural-
sounding words. And then together they
flapped their wings and took off into the sky.
They flew quickly through the city, heading
north across the river, until they came to the

district of Montmartre. Then they swooped straight down towards the Café of Lost Time.

The three gargoyles came crashing through the frosted-glass windows. There were shouts and screams as they swarmed about the ceiling, fluttering their wings furiously. The policemen reached for their guns but the gargoyles dived down and snatched them from their hands.

And then, abruptly, they all stopped, pausing to hover above Mademoiselle Fondue. She looked up to see three hideous, grinning faces licking their stone lips. She made a dash for the door, running out into the street. The policemen followed after – but so did the gargoyles. They swept out through the café windows, grabbed Mademoiselle Fondue and the policemen with their sharp, taloned claws and lifted them, screaming, into the sky.

It was not long after this that the green cloud above the city gradually began to fade. And as it cleared, so did the mist.

The monster in the Seine disappeared with a large ripple and was never to be seen again. The prehistoric skeletons returned to their pedestals, the Sphinx jumped back into her frame and the gargoyles of Notre-Dame returned to the rooftop and became stone statues once more.

By now the streets were crowded. Great

queues of traffic had formed, with people blaring horns and others abandoning their cars, wandering out into the roads. The police were out in force but they seemed just as confused as everybody else and certainly not capable of keeping order. However, there was no violence, for everyone was too awestruck by what they had just seen. And this shared state of wonder seemed to unite them altogether.

Rumours began spreading like wildfire among the crowd. They all agreed that they must have been the victims of a hoax, some kind of spectacular illusion. But who had staged it, or for what purpose, nobody could tell.

Then someone climbed up on to a public monument to address the crowd. 'Look at what they were doing, these creatures, these *gargoyles*,' he said. 'They were saving  our buildings from destruction! Rescuing our beautiful city from this monstrous government. For it is the government who is the true monster!'

Then everyone began marching through the city, chanting: '*Out with the monster! Save our city! Out with the monster! Save our city!*'

They marched along the Champs-Élysées,

until they reached the Presidential Palace. There they called out the President's name and demanded that he resign.

Meanwhile, in the Café of Lost Time, Madame Pamplemousse switched off the machine.

A long silence passed, which was eventually broken by Monsieur Moutarde.

'Bravo, Madame,' he said quietly to Madame Pamplemousse.

'And to you, Monsieur,' she replied with a smile.

'And to Madeleine,' he said, turning towards her. 'A magnificent performance. For a moment I truly believed you were crying real tears.'

'Thank you, Monsieur,' said Madeleine, with a bow.

'Why, naturally,' said Madame Pample-mousse, walking over towards her. 'For Madeleine is one of us — and *people like us should stick together.*'

She stared at Madeleine then, and from the look in her eyes, Madeleine somehow knew that her words held another meaning. One that was intended just for her, and which recalled those words spoken to her by the Sphinx, up on that barren hillside: '*you fear your friends have abandoned you too.*'

Madame Pamplemousse took her by the hand. 'And now, my dear friend,' she said, 'if you would care to accompany me once more, there are some people who would very much like to meet you.'

She lit a candle and then led Madeleine round to the back of the café, where there was a small cellar door. It opened on to an iron stairwell leading down into the dark.

They descended the steps together, until they came out into a long, cavernous tunnel. The only light came from Madame Pamplemousse's flame and Madeleine followed her through the darkness until they stopped before a door. Madame Pamplemousse knocked: a precise series of knocks, like a message in Morse code.

The door opened and they stepped through into a huge candlelit chamber, like an enormous underground dance hall.

People were sitting about at tables lit by flickering candles, and in the corner a trio of musicians was playing jazz. And there, at one of the tables, Madeleine saw two people she recognised: a tall bald man in black leather, who, despite the dimness of the lighting, was wearing dark glasses – it was Monsieur Langoustine, the famous restaurant critic – and sitting opposite him was Camembert.

They were sharing a bottle of wine and, on seeing Madeleine and Madame Pamplemousse, Monsieur Langoustine raised his glass.

Then everyone raised their glasses and a huge cheer went around.

People were applauding and there were shouts of 'Bravo!'

Meanwhile, the musicians continued to play. And it may have been her imagination, or the flickering candlelight, but to Madeleine it seemed that the pianist had stone wings and two little horns on his head.

Epilogue

In France, a new government has since been elected. After mass demonstrations, an emergency election was called and the President subsequently removed from office. The new President promised to revive the old spirit of the country and to restore its capital city. All plans for Paris's demolition were suspended. No longer were its museums and art galleries to become shopping centres. And the heavy taxes on small shops and restaurants were lifted.

To celebrate, the Cornichons took part in a huge street party, with all the restaurants in Paris opening their doors for free. Together, Madeleine and Monsieur Cornichon cooked up an enormous banquet.

Mademoiselle Fondue is no longer involved with politics. She was arrested after being found clinging to the top of the Eiffel Tower. Along with the President, she was brought before a tribunal investigating claims of corruption during their regime. But Mademoiselle Fondue so charmed the judges that she managed to get off on a technicality and, rumour has it, is now working as a model overseas.

However, it is still a mystery what caused the monsters or the green mist, or who the group known only as 'the Gargoyles' really were. But the event has now gone down in history as *la Grande Illusion* and, to commemorate it each year, a special carnival is held.

And on this day,

four friends and old travelling companions always meet up to celebrate and to watch the carnival in the streets outside, from a café high above the city of Paris.

Have you read Madeleine's
other adventures?

Turn the page for an
exciting taster of

MADAME
PAMPLEMOUSSE

AND HER

Incredible Edibles

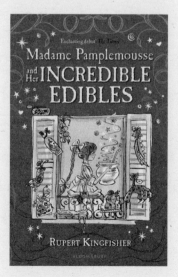

Chapter One

In the city of Paris, on the banks of the river, tucked away from the main street down a narrow, winding alley, there is a shop. A small, rather shabby-looking shop with faded paint-work, a dusty awning and dark, smoky windows. The sign above the door reads 'Edibles', as it is a food shop selling all kinds of rare and exotic delicacies. But they are not just rare and they are not just exotic, for this shop belongs to Madame Pamplemousse, and she sells the strangest, the rarest, the most delicious, the most extraordinary, the most incredible-tasting edibles in all the world.

Inside, the shop is cool and musty-smelling, lit only by candlelight. In the flickering shadows, great bunches of sausages and dried herbs, strings of garlic and chilli peppers, and giant salted meats hang from the ceiling. Rows of cheeses are laid out on beds of dark green leaves and all around there are shelves winding up to the ceiling, crammed with bottles and strangely shaped jars.

Underneath the shop, down a winding spiral staircase, at the end of a long, dark corridor, there is a door. A door that is forever kept locked. For it is behind this door that Madame Pamplemousse cooks her rarest delicacy, a delicacy sold in the tiniest little jar with a label upon which nothing is written. The label is blank and the ingredients are a secret, since it is the single most delicious, the most extraordinary, the most incredible-tasting edible of them all.